Finally Mrs. Darcy

Finally Mrs. Darcy

A Pride and Prejudice Novella

LEENIE BROWN

LEENIE B BOOKS
HALIFAX

Contents

Dedication

To my "evil" influence and wonderful friend,
Rose,
who started me thinking about unhappy end-
ings and setting them right

Prologue

"Are you ready, my dear?"

Elizabeth Amberley, née Bennet, looked up from the trunk she was packing and nodded. It was the expected answer and won her a smile from her aunt.

"It will not be so bad. It is a second chance at happiness."

Again Elizabeth nodded, but in her heart, she could not agree. Her chance at true happiness had been lost long ago. Five years ago to be exact. She had attempted a second chance at happiness once already only to find herself merely contented and then, within a short period of time, a widow.

"I do not plan to remarry, Aunt."

Maria Amberly wrapped an arm around Elizabeth's shoulder. "So I have told your uncle, but he is convinced that you shall change your mind."

She chuckled. "And I have learned that when Gareth Amberly is bent on a plan, be it political or personal, there is very little which will stop him. He is quite unlike Jack in that regard." She crossed the room to the window and looked across the open fields toward where Netherfield stood in the distance. "Even as a boy, Jack was malleable. He would take an idea into his head and then upon hearing a friend's, his plan would change." She looked back at Elizabeth. "I dare say it was quite different for you."

Elizabeth joined her aunt at the window. She would miss this view when she was in town, but the estate was no longer hers now that Jack was dead. "I fear you are right. My will could be quite unyielding as a child. Even as a young woman I struggled with accepting anyone's ideas as right save my own."

Her aunt laughed. "My dear, you are still a young woman, which is why you deserve a second chance at happiness."

Elizabeth's smile was tight. "I think I have had my share of happiness. Perhaps it is another's chance now and not mine."

"You were happy with Jack?" The question was

soft almost as if her aunt were fearful of knowing the truth.

Elizabeth nodded. Being content, as she had been with Jack, was not unhappiness; it was just not so fulfilling as she imagined it could be.

Her aunt studied Elizabeth's face, then, with a nod, she turned to leave. "A season will do you good. There will be sights to see, soirees to attend, and new clothes in colours other than those of mourning to purchase. And your uncle has already been making a list of acquaintances to whom he wishes to introduce you."

Elizabeth sighed.

"It is not very long — yet." Her aunt chuckled. "He claims the best prospects will be at your first soiree, and if none of them take, he will then revise his list."

Elizabeth shook her head. "I do not plan to remarry," she repeated.

"Pah," her aunt waved the words away, "you may find your opinion swayed. Do not close your mind to the possibility." She winked at Elizabeth as she left the room and calling to a footman to attend to the trunk that Elizabeth's maid had just closed.

"She is persistent," Elizabeth said to the maid.

"That she is, ma'am."

"But they are very kind."

"Indeed, ma'am, I have always thought so."

Elizabeth tipped her head and looked at the young girl whom she had selected to attend her after she married. "Are you ready for the town, Grace? It is very different from Hertfordshire."

"I am, ma'am."

Elizabeth turned toward the window again. "Will you miss your family?" Her thoughts roamed first to the little plot of earth in the church-yard where her own father now rested and then to the cottage not far from Aunt Philips where Mama and Kitty now lived, ending finally at the rooms above a shop where Mary happily tended to her family while her husband saw to his customers below. She would miss this. Jane, happily, would be in town for, at least, the season.

"I suppose I shall, ma'am, but my home is with you."

Elizabeth gave her a small smile.

"And a happy home it has been and will be," Grace added. "Is there anything else, ma'am?"

"No. You should go see to your things."

"Thank you, ma'am." Grace dipped a curtsey

and left the room, leaving Elizabeth a few moments of solitude before a footman came to collect the trunk, and her aunt returned to hurry her along to the carriage.

Elizabeth gave the room a final look before turning to leave. In her heart, she said a prayer of thanks for the man who had provided this for her and given her connections to wonderful relatives such as Gareth and Maria Amberly. Then with another prayer for patience to endure the scheming of her uncle, she descended the stairs to the waiting carriage and what was to be her new life.

Chapter 1

Elizabeth took in the splendor of the ballroom. It was far grander than she had ever experienced. The walls were decorated with portraits and landscapes, one standing alongside the next with others over and below them. Four large chandeliers twinkled, their brilliance reflected in several mirrors that hung amongst the paintings. Down the length of the room to her left, doors opened into the house, while on her right were grand doors framed by pillars and heavy drapes leading into the garden. At the far end of the room, a small group of musicians was pausing between dances, and on the floor, only a few chalk flowers remained distinguishable. She no longer felt overdressed, though, she did still feel strange wearing colour after so long in mourning clothes.

"Come, my dear." Her uncle, Gareth Amberly, took her elbow. "There are people to meet."

Elizabeth put a smile on her face and nodded. At one time she had enjoyed meeting people. It had been amusing to watch their interactions and make judgments about their character, but that was before she had discovered how very little she knew about judging character.

They had stopped about half way down the length of the left side of the room. Her uncle lifted onto his toes, stretching his neck this way and that as if searching for someone in particular. Inwardly, Elizabeth sighed and turned to admire a painting of a young woman with a small child on her lap and another standing just behind her shoulder. Uncle Gareth had been eagerly talking about this ball for a fortnight. He was worse than Lydia for excitement and equalled her mother for chatter about of this or that gentleman. She tilted her head and wistfully examined the face of the young child. No matter how she might long for a family of her own, Uncle Gareth was far more eager to see her remarried than she was. Although her time in town had helped her spirits to lift and a small glimmer of hope that happiness might be possible, she truly had no desire to marry again...unless... She shook her head. That was hopeless. She had had her chance and squandered it. She was certain that Mr. Darcy had married long ago and to someone more acceptable than she. She would have to be content with spoiling her nieces and nephews instead of her own children. The thought saddened her, but she would not marry again unless she could give her heart completely. And that was just simply impossible. She turned away from the painting just as her uncle turned to her with a pleased smile.

"Ah, there is someone for you to meet." Mr. Amberly was once again steering her by the elbow through the crowds of people.

Although she longed to be anywhere but here in a bustling ballroom being introduced to gentlemen, she could not help her small giggle at his excitement. He was a dear man, and she would meet anyone he deemed worthy of the introduction.

"He is older but has never married." Her uncle, leaned close and, as if not wishing to be heard by his quarry, spoke in hushed tones. "Some say he has been nursing a broken heart for years so I'd not get my hopes up, but one never knows." He gave her a wink. "And you must start somewhere. You are too young to remain a widow. You need a husband and children. Jack was a good man, but he is not the only good man. In fact, I wondered at times if he really was the man for you." He patted her arm reassuringly. "Oh, I know you were happy, but — and I probably should not speak so of my own nephew — there was something missing — a glow, a sparkle." He patted her arm once again. "You were not designed for such a dull existence."

Elizabeth blushed at the comment, for he was quite correct. Her marriage had been a happy one. Both husband and wife were good-natured and well-suited in temperament, but it was a dull existence. Jack would never cross Elizabeth in debate no matter how often she attempted to engage him, and he would never do anything to provoke. Though he found many things diverting, none was ever diverting enough to truly enjoy a good laugh — the kind that caused joy to bubble up and overwhelm your soul, that caused you to gasp for air and brush away tears. But, he had provided a good home, a good income, and good connections. Even after his passing, she had been surrounded by those who truly cared for her. She knew she should be thankful for such an arrangement — and truly she was. She was content to be in such a secure position as she now was, but there was a part of her that longed for more...what was the word? Her cheeks flushed further as her mind found it. *Passion* — she longed for more passion in life.

"Here we are." Her uncle tapped a gentleman on the shoulder.

Elizabeth gasped, and her free hand flew to her heart as the man turned around.

"Ah, Mr. Darcy, may I present my niece, Mrs. Amberly. Elizabeth, dear, this is Mr. Darcy of Pemberley in Derbyshire." Her uncle hid a small smile as he took in the looks of astonishment on both faces. Perhaps the rumours he had heard were true. He waited a few moments for one or the other to speak, but seeing that it was unlikely, he prodded, "I had hoped you might be willing to dance with Elizabeth, Mr. Darcy. This is her first social event since she came out of mourning."

"Mourning?" Darcy blinked and slowly shifted his gaze to the man next to Elizabeth. He struggled to remember the man's name. He had met him once or twice. Had his uncle introduced the man to him?

Mr. Amberly nodded. "My nephew — died of a trifling cold that turned into a raging fever."

"My condolences to you both." Amberly, her name, as well as the gentleman's, was Amberly. His gaze shifted from Mr. Amberly to Elizabeth.

"Thank you, Mr. Darcy." Elizabeth's voice was soft and wavered just a bit. "It came as a shock to have one so young taken so quickly. My father's passing was less shocking."

"Your father, too?" She had lost both a husband and a father? In all of his thinking about her, he had not once imagined so great a loss befalling her. No, his thoughts had always tended to see her happy with her sisters and father. He had supposed she would marry, but he never allowed the thought to occupy his mind for any length of time — the pain of such a thing was too great.

"The month prior," said Elizabeth.

"Ah, but Elizabeth is here tonight to put much of that behind her." Mr. Amberly smiled at Mr. Darcy. He had brought Elizabeth to this ball to meet this man to restore her happiness, and talk of dead husbands and fathers was not going to do it. A dance, a time to reminisce about a previous acquaintance, that was what was needed. "Not that a dance can make you forget those who have been lost," he explained, "but it can help us move forward. Our lives simply must not stop because another's life has ended." He moved slightly so that Elizabeth was closer to Darcy and looked expectantly at the gentleman.

"I fear my uncle will be quite disappointed if we do not dance, sir." Elizabeth smiled at her uncle and then returned her attention to Darcy. "I would be honoured to dance with you if I am still acceptable as a partner. I realize it has been five years since we last saw each other, but I think I can still qualify as a person known to you and not one of those less tolerable sort." She leaned a bit closer and whispered. "Strangers."

Her uncle could not hide his smile at that. It had been years since he had witnessed her lively wit. The absence of that wit was what first caused him to doubt the strength of the bond between her and his nephew. "May I leave her in your care, Mr. Darcy, and seek out my wife before she has engaged herself for every dance? I do not wish to be left standing about like an old fool?"

"You may." Darcy gave a small bow of acceptance.

Mr. Amberly winked at Elizabeth and squeezed her elbow reassuringly before weaving his way through the crowd to find his wife.

An awkward silence filled her uncle's place. A few people jostled passed them before Darcy spoke.

"Come, Mrs. Amberly, we must have some conversation. I hear it is required even in a ballroom."

Elizabeth giggled behind her fan. "Shall we speak of books?"

He extended his arm to her as the music began. "Books should never be spoken of in a ballroom, and I would rather hear about you." They took their place in line.

She glanced at the people beside her. "I doubt, sir, that here is the best place for such a conversation."

He smiled, ignoring her suggestion. He did not wish to speak about the weather or some other trivial matter especially when he longed to hear about her. "Your sisters? Are they well?"

The music began and drew them together for a moment before sending them apart.

"They are," she said as they came together again. "All save Kitty are married, but we expect a happy announcement shortly — or at least Uncle Gareth does. He is ever the optimist." She stepped away and then back. "I, however, think it will be yet one more season before Kitty is settled. Four and twenty tends to turn a young woman's mind to seriously contemplating marriage before her bloom has faded."

As she wove her way in and out, she thought of how turning that age had inspired her to consider marriage without strong affection. The fear of being a burden to her family or worse, being left to scratch out a meager existence on her own, had caused her mother's desire to see her daughters married and Charlotte's choice to marry Mr. Collins understandable. And so, when Jack had presented his offer, it seemed only logical to accept. He did not claim to love her, but he did respect her. Feeling it was the best she would be able to manage, having already lost the one who held her heart, she had agreed.

Their hands met again. "Lydia is also married as you well know."

He blinked and halted his steps nearly causing

another gentleman to stumble. "And why would I know that?"

She lifted an eyebrow and stared up at him. "Because, you were there, sir." She smiled. "Lydia cannot keep a secret, and when she and her husband visited Longbourn, she mentioned your attendance at her wedding. I admit that bit of information piqued my curiosity and my mind would not rest until I ferreted out the remaining information from my aunt Gardiner." She looked away from his eyes for a moment. She wished to ask him why he had done so much for her sister and yet cut all ties to her family, but her heart faltered as a couple wound their way past her. So, instead, she said what she had wished to say those five years ago. "I must thank you on behalf of my family."

Upon returning her gaze to him, she was startled to find a pained expression in his eyes. Thinking that in speaking of the incident, she may have spoken amiss, she was about to apologize when Darcy swiftly took her by the hand and led her out of the line, behind one of the columns next to the garden door and onto the terrace.

"You were right." He said as they took the steps

which led to the garden. "The dance floor was not the best place for such a conversation." He placed her hand on his arm as they descended the steps and began down a path. "My actions toward your sister and Mr. Wickham were to salve my own conscience by guaranteeing you would not be harmed through my lack of openness regarding Mr. Wickham's lack of character." He stopped and looked at her. "I believe, I thought only of you."

She shook her head in disbelief. How could he say such a thing? She had hoped that he had helped Lydia for her sake, but then, when Mr. Bingley had returned to Netherfield alone and said his connection with Mr. Darcy was at an end, her hope had faded. It was as she had first feared, he wanted nothing to do with a family who was so shamefully tied to Mr. Wickham.

"Why?" The question would not go unasked. "Why would you think so highly of me, and yet not..." She turned away. "Why did you not return?" She closed her eyes and attempted to prepare herself for whatever excuse he might give. She did not have a wish to hear his reason. It was something far more demanding. It was a need. She needed to know the truth for good or for ill.

Darcy watched her wrap her arms around her-self and take one step away from him. "I spoke to Bingley shortly after Miss Lydia married Wick-ham." He closed the distance between them. "I attempted to confess all that I had done to separate him from Miss Bennet, but he only heard half before he refused to listen further and stormed from my home." The dirt on the path crunched lightly as he dug his toe into it.

"It was not because of Lydia?" It was a shocking thought, for she had never considered any other possibility.

"No," Darcy replied firmly. "It was because of me. Bingley has had no contact with me since, other than to return my letters unopened and request that I not contact him or any of his family. By that time, you were included in that group, since he and your sister were married. So, I stayed away hoping that by doing as he requested, he might, at some point, forgive me. I continue to wait."

"He speaks of you." Elizabeth gave a quick glance over her shoulder. "Since Papa died. You may not have much longer to wait."

"I have waited for an eternity, Elizabeth, and it

has cost me dearly." The depth of the pain in his words pierced her heart.

"When you did not return with Bingley, I thought it was because you did not wish to be associated with a family tied to Mr. Wickham or such foolish girls as Lydia — and who could blame you?" She turned to face him. "It broke my heart. I refused to attend assemblies for nearly a year. Mama thought it was because I missed Jane, but it was you I missed." She took one of his hands. "Eventually, I could no longer refuse to attend, and I met Jack. He was a pleasant man. He smiled much and spoke well of all he met. I believe he was constitutionally incapable of being disagreeable. He respected me, and I was happy, but he was not you." She squeezed his hand. "I loved him, but not as I love you."

"You love me?" Darcy stood perfectly still. His breath caught in his chest as he waited for her reply. The thought that his affections might be returned threatened to make him embarrass himself by either causing him to weep or shout or, heaven forbid, both.

"For these five long years, I have loved you. I have tried not to, but it is impossible. I fear I shall always love you." A breeze tugged a wisp of hair free, and she brushed it away from her face. "It is why I have told my uncle I do not wish to marry again — not that he will hear of that, but it was not fair to Jack and would not be fair to another to give him only part of me."

"You love me." Thankfully, his delight only spread across his face and did not express itself with any more exuberance than that.

She nodded.

"Are you certain you will never marry again?" He stepped closer to her, looked into her eyes and brushed that wayward wisp of hair from her cheek.

"Never." She drew the hand she held around her waist. "Unless it is you."

"You will marry me?" Again, the happiness of his heart wished to be released in a cry of victory, but he would not allow it.

"If you will have me." She smiled up at him as his arms pulled her close.

"You will marry me." He bent his head to kiss her softly. "My feelings and wishes have never changed. I love you now as I loved you then, most ardently."

Elizabeth drew his mouth back down to hers.

These were the kisses for which she had longed. The kind of kiss that sent fire racing through her body from her lips all the way down to her toes. The kind of kiss that caused her to long for greater intimacy.

"Elizabeth," he whispered near her ear as he pressed kisses along her neck. "When? When will you marry me?"

She sighed and held him tightly to her. "This very moment if it were possible."

"I shall acquire a special license. One week," he claimed her lips once again, "one week, and you shall be mine."

Chapter 2

"Fitzwilliam."

A voice broke through the delicious haze that surrounded Darcy as he held Elizabeth.

"Fitzwilliam."

A hand tugged at his coat. His eyes flew open, and he released Elizabeth as he realized just where he was and who was calling to him.

Elizabeth peeked around his arm and saw a pretty young lady of about twenty, who wore a lovely pale blue gown and a very amused smile. "Your sister?" Elizabeth whispered.

"Georgiana," said Darcy with a nod, straightening his jacket before he turned to face his sister.

"I was afraid you were sitting in the garden feeling melancholy as you normally do after an hour of standing about watching me." Georgiana leaned to her right to see around her brother and smiled at Elizabeth. "But, I see you were not."

"You remember Miss Elizabeth?" Darcy took Elizabeth's hand and drew her forward. "Although, she is no longer Miss Elizabeth; she is Mrs. Amberly."

Georgiana's eyes grew wide. "Mrs. Amberly? You are married?"

"I was, but my husband died last year." She accepted Georgiana's words of sympathy and glanced uneasily at Darcy. "I know this looks horrible. It is not at all proper."

The amused look Georgiana had worn only moments ago, returned to her face. "Indeed." The word was nearly a laugh, and her smile completely ruined the effect of the scowl she attempted as she looked at her brother.

Darcy looked at Elizabeth and then his sister, but, instead of becoming flustered or stern as both ladies might have expected, a smile split his face. "We should go back."

"You may wish to allow Mrs. Amberly a few moments to...um...look less ravished," suggested Georgiana as she tried to stifle a laugh.

"I did not ravish her," Darcy retorted, turning

to look at Elizabeth. Her cheeks were rosy and her hair, which had been perfectly arranged, was looking rather disheveled. He chuckled. "Although, I do admit she does look it."

"You needn't sound so proud of yourself, Fitzwilliam." Georgiana swatted his arm as she moved to Elizabeth's side and slipped her arm around Elizabeth's. "I saw a bench just down this path. A few moments in the cool air will help your cheeks, and I can assist you with your hair." She lifted an eyebrow and gave her brother a disapproving look. "I should be shocked and disappointed," she said over her shoulder, "but I am too pleased to see you smiling to scold."

"I am sorry," said Elizabeth softly.

Georgiana leaned closer and patted her arm. "You need not apologize. I have not seen him stand so straight or smile so broadly in years. And," she glanced over her shoulder at her brother, "I think he will have to be more forgiving of my errors from this point forward." She laughed when he cleared his throat in disapproval. "Oh, do not worry, Fitzwilliam, I know you are a man and Mrs. Amberly is a widow so society raises fewer eyebrows at such behavior for you than for a maiden like me."

"Oh," cried Elizabeth. "It was not like that!" She sat down on the bench and looked at Darcy. She wanted to tell Georgiana of their understanding, that this was not some clandestine meeting, but she did not feel it was her place.

"Georgiana," Darcy's stern tone had returned, but the smile had not left his face. He knew he was grinning foolishly, but Elizabeth had agreed to marry him, and the long-denied desire of his heart was soon to be fulfilled, so it really could not be helped. "I had hoped to speak to Elizabeth's uncle first, but since you must have an explanation, Elizabeth has agreed to be my wife. I know it is rather sudden —."

Georgiana's laugh interrupted him. "Sudden? You have been pining for Miss Elizabeth for years." She had taken a small comb from her reticule and had set about restoring Elizabeth's coiffure as best she could.

"Georgiana!" Darcy's voice was still stern.

"Do not worry, Brother, I shall not tell her of your desolation." She chuckled at his growl.

"There." She tucked one last strand of hair back in place. "You look presentable."

"Beautiful," murmured Darcy, causing his sister's smile to widen and her eyes to sparkle with tears.

Elizabeth felt her cheeks, which had just begun to cool, grow warm once again.

"It might be best if we remain here for a few moments and then return, you and I arm in arm, and my brother a respectable distance behind." Georgiana sat down next to Elizabeth and patted the spot next to her in invitation to her brother. "Widowed or no, we should do our best to quell any rumours that might spread." She tilted her head and looked at Darcy. "I assume you took care when leaving the ballroom together to not be obvious?" She shook her head at her brother's groan. "So you were not. That does present a wrinkle, but returning as I suggested should appease many of the gossipmongers." She giggled, clearly delighting in her brother's discomfort.

It truly did not matter how they returned. The news of Mr. Darcy marrying would be enough for tongues to wag and the curious to call. "There will be a price to pay, of course, when your marriage becomes known. Society has commented on your single state for so long that to have it suddenly altered will be of great interest. I would suggest removing the knocker if you do not wish to be flooded with callers." She smoothed her skirts. "How long until the wedding?"

"A week." Elizabeth's reply was soft, and she feared her cheeks would never cool.

"If I can acquire a license within that time and procure her uncle's blessing," Darcy added.

"A week?" Georgiana looked between the two with wide eyes. "Why not be off to Gretna Green within the hour and be done with it?" There was a teasing tone to her voice.

"I have waited five years, Georgiana, so I will thank you not to tease me about my impatience."

His sister placed her hand on his arm. "I am so very happy for you, Fitzwilliam." She placed her other hand on Elizabeth's arm. "For both of you."

"Should we return?" asked Elizabeth.

"As long as you will walk about the room with me and tell me of yourself and your family while my brother seeks out your uncle," said Georgiana.

"But do you not have partners waiting for you?" The thought that a lady so beautiful and rich as Georgiana would not have partners for every dance baffled Elizabeth.

Georgiana pulled out her dance card and showed it to Elizabeth. "There are two real gentlemen listed, and of course, my brother, but I do not care for dancing."

Elizabeth laughed, and Georgiana joined her.

"Does your brother approve? I had once heard he deplored all sorts of disguise."

Georgiana leaned a bit closer. "He would rather I remain home and neither dance nor attend these soirees, but since I must find a husband..." She shrugged. "To my knowledge, it is the only disguise he condones. But do not worry, I have heard the lecture on how dishonesty can lead to disastrous consequences, ones which can alter the course of one's life."

"The loss of a friend and a love," Darcy said softly. "Disastrous is too gentle a word, in all honesty."

Georgiana's hand flew to her mouth. "Oh!" Her eyes grew wide. "That lecture has something to do with you?" She looked at Elizabeth.

"And Bingley," added Darcy.

"Your parting of ways?"

Darcy nodded and then sighed. "Thinking I was doing Bingley a service, I kept information from him. However, I was neither doing him a service nor was it for me to decide what information he knew or did not know. I overstepped my bounds."

Georgiana's brows drew together. "I can certainly see how that would damage a friendship, but I am uncertain as to how Mrs. Amberly is involved."

"Bingley married my sister Jane," said Elizabeth.

Georgiana blinked and pursed her lips, obviously attempting to reconcile that bit of information with what her brother had said and not succeeding.

"Bingley informed me," said Darcy, "that he never wished to see or hear from me again. He demanded that I keep my distance from his family, which included Elizabeth."

Understanding suffused Georgiana's face and filled her eyes with sadness as she looked first at her brother and then Elizabeth. "How could you bear it?"

"I had no choice," said Darcy. He studied his hands. How many times had he considered defying

Bingley's demands? If he had felt assured of Elizabeth's affections, nothing would have kept him from her. But, until tonight when she had declared her love for him, he had not been certain.

Elizabeth drew her bottom lip between her teeth to keep it from trembling as it wished. The pain of those first few months when he did not return could not be hidden and etched its way across her features.

Georgiana wrapped her arms around Elizabeth's shoulders. "Oh, my dear, I am so very sorry."

"As am I," muttered Darcy.

"What is done cannot be undone," said Elizabeth with a sad shrug and a small shake of her head. "Just like the water in the river that flows to the sea, it is gone and cannot be brought back, but new water takes its place. Soon these painful thoughts will be but a distant memory." She drew a deep breath and stood. "Tomorrow, I will write to my sister and share my good news, but tonight, I will gladly walk with you, Georgiana, and tell you of my sisters and my nieces and nephews."

She held out her hand to Georgiana, who took it and rose. Elizabeth looked at Darcy as she and

Georgiana joined arms. "Jane and Bingley have three, two girls and a little boy, who is doted on by his older sisters and his mama."

She turned, and they started walking. "Mary, my next youngest sister, married not long after I did and is expecting her first child in the fall. Her husband, Anthony, opened his sweets shop in Meryton about three years ago and has been very successful. Mama was a trifle disappointed that he was not a landed gentleman, but her expectations for Mary were never high."

Darcy trailed after his sister and Elizabeth, listening to the discussion, and, although his heart was overjoyed to have Elizabeth accept him, it was also grieved by all he had missed in the past five years. Bingley had daughters and an heir? If Darcy had not chased after Wickham when he eloped with Lydia, if he had confessed his part in separating Bingley from Jane, if he had merely travelled to Netherfield with his friend and given his approval of a renewed acquaintance with Miss Bennet, might this be his lot now? Would he have had five happy years with Elizabeth and children of his own? He briefly closed his eyes and shook his head, overwhelmed at the thought of having had so much taken from him.

They were approaching the entrance to the ballroom, so he stopped. When Elizabeth looked back at him in question, he smiled and gave a small wave of his hand, indicating that she should continue on without him.

She returned his smile but hesitated.

Georgiana gave Elizabeth's arm a small tug. "We must enter separately," she whispered.

Elizabeth knew that leaving him now was only for a short time and quite necessary to keep her reputation from being tarnished, but her heart did not completely care about the logic of the plan. It wanted to stay with him. It had no desire to ever let him out of her sight, and when she turned away, it protested loudly. But with one last look over her shoulder in his direction, she allowed herself to be led inside to begin a slow circuit of the room.

Darcy clenched his fists at his side and counted slowly to twenty as he willed his feet to remain where they were until Elizabeth and his sister were well into the ballroom. Then, drawing in a deep breath and releasing it slowly, he made his way to the edge of the crowd. Georgiana had not been wrong. Many eyes were following Elizabeth and his sister as they walked, and several turned his direction when he entered. He did his best to ignore them as he scanned the room, looking for Elizabeth's uncle. The search was not a long one. Mr. Amberly must have been watching the door for his return, for the man was already making his way across the room towards Darcy.

Darcy chuckled. His height not only made it easier for him to see above the heads of many of the guests in attendance, but it also made it far easier for others to find him. He pulled his watch from his pocket and noted the time as he waited for Mr. Amberly to reach him. It was not altogether extra-ordinarily late. Although his solicitor might find it so, and he was certain the Archbishop would not like a visit at this hour. However, he thought with a smile as he returned his watch to his pocket, at least one of the unfortunate fellows was surely going to be put out with him tonight.

Georgiana would be dancing the fourth set with Mr. Murrish and then leaving. Darcy had noted that Mr. Murrish was the only gentleman his sister looked for at each soiree, so Darcy was confi-dent that so long as he did not make his sister miss her dance with the man, she would not mind leaving early. Or — his smile grew as a pleasant thought crossed his mind — perhaps he could leave his sister to the care of Elizabeth.

"It is warm in here, is it not, Mr. Darcy?" Mr. Amberly asked as he approached. "I thought I might take a bit of air while my wife is otherwise occupied. She likes to dance every set if she can." He stepped out the door and turned. "Come, join me."

Darcy smiled at how Mr. Amberly was making it his idea to speak with Darcy instead of Darcy seeking him out.

"I thought there might be less talk this way," explained Mr. Amberly.

"It is appreciated."

"The room is already a flutter with the news of you sneaking off into the garden with a widow. The stories that have surfaced in such a short time are entertaining when you know they are not true." He smiled at Darcy. "I know your character, Mr. Darcy, as does everyone in that room. But, I also know how a disappointed woman's mind can work and her tongue can cut." He leaned against the balustrades of the porch and chuckled. "I do not wish to be the lady who says such things within the hearing of my niece. She is quite the expert at a set down. Oh, she has not had the opportunity to use those skills in town yet, but she has had plenty of practice in Hertfordshire." He glanced at Darcy. "My nephew's estate was ten miles from Longbourn and thirteen from Netherfield. There is a well-travelled road that connects them. And Elizabeth and Jack attended every assembly and at least one ball at Netherfield. Jack loved to dance nearly as much as, I imagine, Elizabeth once did."

Elizabeth's uncle stared off into the ballroom, and he lapsed into silence for a moment. Then he returned his focus back to Darcy and their conversation, though his eyes did not leave the dancers. "I purposefully brought her here tonight, Mr. Darcy. I had heard the rumors of your having lost a love some years back." He shrugged. "I started piecing things together, making small inquiries and watching reactions. I heard tales of an Elizabeth that I rarely got to see. I heard how she used to dance every dance, even if she had to stand up with her sisters, and how she used to challenge people with her wit."

"Used to?" asked Darcy. "Does she not still do

so?" Such an Elizabeth as Mr. Amberly described both shocked and saddened him.

Mr. Amberly shook his head and turned toward Darcy, so that one hip rested against the rail. "It changed, I understand, not long after Lydia was married, and Mr. Bingley returned to Netherfield. People attributed the change to having two sisters married before her. According to Jane, Elizabeth endured a particularly long period of melancholy, but even Jane was not sure as to the cause." He tapped his nose and smiled. "But I think I know." He shifted and leaned his weight more fully against the balustrades. "Elizabeth cared for my nephew, but she never fully gave him her heart. And my guess is that it is because she had given it to you long ago." He chuckled at Darcy's look of surprise.

"You knew she loved me?"

Mr. Amberly lifted his left shoulder in a shrug while tipping his head towards it as if to say it was not so difficult to figure out what he had. "When do you marry?"

Darcy shook his head in disbelief. "In a week's time if I can procure a license and have contracts prepared." He could not contain the grin that spread across his face at the thought. "That is if we have your permission."

"She is old enough to marry without it, but you have both my permission and my blessing." Mr. Amberly pulled a slip of paper from his pocket. "This is my solicitor's name and address. He has all the papers necessary on Elizabeth's behalf for the transaction to be completed as quickly as possible. Like I said, Mr. Darcy, I came here tonight with the intent of seeing her happy."

Chapter 3

Darcy looked up from his cup of coffee. A freshly pressed and folded newspaper lay beside his plate just as it had been placed there earlier by a footman in anticipation of his master's regular habit of reading it as he had his breakfast. But this morning, Darcy was not interested in the paper. His mind was more pleasantly occupied with thoughts of marriage contracts and, of course, Elizabeth. He was quite enjoying his reverie when his sister entered.

"You needn't look so surprised, Fitzwilliam." Georgiana took a seat next to him.

"You are rarely up so early after a soiree, dear sister." He tipped his head to the side and gave her an inquiring look.

"I usually do not leave soirees so early," she said

with a smile. "Was your solicitor overly put out to be roused at such an hour?"

He chuckled and returned his attention to his cup. "Not as much as the Archbishop."

She shook her head. "It is not wise to irritate those from whom you wish favours. You could have waited until today and applied as everyone else does."

"What good are relations with connections if you cannot occasionally use them," said Darcy with a shrug. He rarely bandied about his uncle's name, for there was normally no need of it. However, last night when the door to the Archbishop's residence was about to close on him without his request being met, he had decided to use whatever weapons he had at his disposal to acquire that which he needed. And a hasty marriage license was needed.

Georgiana took a sip of her tea. "Will Uncle Matlock be pleased to hear that you were throwing his name about at ungodly hours?"

Darcy shrugged again. "He has been pestering me to marry for some time. I should think he would be delighted to know I have finally agreed to do so."

Georgiana swirled her tea gently in her cup. "She is not what he would have recommended," she said softly.

Darcy sighed. "I am aware of that, but he has no sway over my decision." He had allowed his relations' opinions to colour his own at one point, and it had cost him dearly. Had he not listened to that inner voice warning him of family expectations, he might have succeeded with Elizabeth at Hunsford.

"He may make things unpleasant for Elizabeth when he visits."

"Then he shall not visit," Darcy said firmly. There was not a reason nor a relative in the world that would sway him from marrying Elizabeth.

Georgiana bit back a smile. "Do you mean it? Might we also not have to visit Aunt Catherine?"

"You needn't sound so happy," he replied with a chuckle. "However, I would not be saddened by the thought." He swallowed the last of his coffee and stood. "I did not dare rouse Mr. Amberly's solicitor last night, so I am off to see him at his earliest convenience, and I shall not return until he has found it convenient to see me. What are your plans for today?"

Georgiana sighed as if her day was going to be dull and took a slow sip of her tea. "Elizabeth is coming this morning, and after I give her a small tour of the house, the modiste will be arriving. Mrs. Amberly will need some new clothes for when she receives her new name."

"Elizabeth is coming here?" He had taken his seat again.

Georgiana nodded.

"You are giving her a tour?"

Georgiana nodded again.

"Without me?"

"That was the plan," she said with a smile.

"It is not a very good one," he muttered. "Perhaps it is best if I just send a note to inquire as to when Mr. Amberly's solicitor is available to see me."

Georgiana shook her head. "That will not do, Fitzwilliam. Time is of the essence in seeing that all is arranged if you wish to marry next week."

Darcy sank back in his chair. What his sister said was true. As much as he wished to be present for Elizabeth's tour of Darcy House, he also did not wish to slow the arrangements that needed to be made.

"She will be here on the half hour. It is only a few minutes. Why do you not wait to depart until after she has arrived?" suggested Georgiana. "You may tell her good morning, and I shall avert my eyes so you may kiss her, and then you can be off." She giggled at the glare he gave her. "You know you wish me to avert my eyes. I am only suggesting it because I know it is what you desire."

"Your fluttering lashes will not work with me, Georgiana. You are not quite so innocent as you appear."

She smiled widely at the comment. "I am certain I do not comprehend your meaning."

He shook his head and rose to leave. "I will delay my departure for a few minutes," he said as he bent to kiss the top of her head.

"Do you wish me to ask all the servants who gather to turn about when you kiss her?"

He placed a finger under her chin and tilted her face up to look at his, the scowl he wore quickly fading to a grin. "It might be best," he said with a wink.

She laughed and wrapped her arms around his waist, pulling him to her. "I have missed your teasing," she said. "I had almost forgotten you knew how."

"Have I been so terrible?" he asked in concern. His right hand rested on her right shoulder with his thumb brushing back and forth across her arm.

She shook her head and released him. "Not terrible, Brother. You could never be terrible. You are far too caring to be so," she gave him a smile, "even to Aunt Catherine." She took his left hand. "But you have been sad, excessively serious — even for you — and despondent even. I had thought it was the rift between you and Mr. Bingley that caused it. I did not realize it was more than the loss of a friend."

"Indeed, it was a great deal more," he said softly. He gave her shoulder a pat before removing his hand. He sighed. He knew that at some point he was going to have to face that friend once again, but presently, he had no desire to do so.

"Do you hate him?" Georgiana tilted her head as she always did when studying something closely.

Darcy returned to his seat. Speaking of his thoughts and feelings was not something he had ever enjoyed doing, but he knew the look on his sister's face. She would have an answer either now or sometime in the future. And since it seemed better to have it over and done with, he expelled a breath, shook his head, and began.

"I do not know. I have hated him. Every time I have stood in a ballroom or sat at a musicale or wandered the museum and watched the happiness of the people around me, I have despised him." He shrugged. "But happiness has found me at last, despite Bingley's interference, and now I am unsure how to think of him." He shrugged. "I suppose some would say I should forgive him while others would have me shun him. I am unsure I can do either. He is married to Elizabeth's sister so refusing to see him would harm her, and that I will not do. However —."

"Your good opinion, once lost, is difficult to restore," interrupted Georgiana.

Darcy nodded his agreement and then shrugged. "Time will tell, I suppose."

Georgiana placed her empty tea cup on the table and looked at the clock. "It is almost time to receive our caller." She smiled at him. "You will do what is right," she assured him. "You always do. Now, have you told the staff that they are to have a new mistress?" She patted his hand and chuckled.

"I can see from the look on your face you have not. Shall I introduce her to them as a friend until you have had the chance?"

"No. I shall speak to Mr. Palmer and Mrs. Cole straightaway." He stood once more to leave. "I shan't be long." He nodded to the footman that stood near the door as he passed through it. Then, with a shake of his head, he turned back to address the man. "You must not tell Mr. Palmer or Mrs. Cole that I told you first, but since you have no doubt heard much of our conversation this morning, you should know that I am getting married."

"Congratulations, sir," replied the footman, a faint smile forming on his otherwise well-schooled features.

"Not that I do not trust your skills completely, Sam, but I do wish to make the best possible impression."

"Of course, sir." He gave a nod of his head. "I will inform the others as soon as I have completed my duties here, sir."

Darcy shook his head. "Tell them first and then come back for the dishes. Mrs. Amberly will be here very soon. Oh, and if you see Mrs. Cole or Mr.

Palmer when you are on your way, tell them I wish to speak to them. I shall be waiting near the door."

"Right away, sir." A smile flashed across Sam's face before he could stop it.

Darcy thanked him and hurried out of the dining room.

Two minutes later, as Darcy peered through the window next to the door for the third time, Mr. Palmer and Mrs. Cole joined him.

"You wished to see us, sir?" asked Mr. Palmer.

"Indeed, I do," said Darcy, turning to face them. These two had been with him since he was a boy. They were more family than servants, and yet, he attempted to keep the distinction as clear as possible. However, there were times, such as now, that it was nearly impossible. "I am getting married," he said with a smile. "Next week," he added.

"Next week, sir?" Mrs. Cole's eyes fluttered slightly in surprise.

"It is sudden, I suppose." His smile grew in size. He was certain that, at any moment, he was going to make a complete and total fool of himself as his excitement at finally having gained Elizabeth was nearly overwhelming. "But it is also not sudden."

Mr. Palmer's brows furrowed.

"I promise to share the full story with you at a later time. However, for now, I shall tell you that I met her six years ago and would have married her then if events had not prevented it." He peered out the window again. "I met her again at last night's ball." He chuckled. "I nearly completed a full dance with her before we came to an understanding." He could see by the looks on their faces that his servants clearly thought he had gone mad. "I assure you that I have not lost control of my mental faculties."

"Does she have a name, sir?" Mrs. Cole asked as Darcy peered out the window once again.

"Elizabeth Amberly," he said. "Mrs. Amberly — she is a widow." He clapped his hands and turned away from the window. "She is here. Georgiana is to give her a tour of the house."

"I will inform the staff," said Mrs. Cole. "Is everything to be open to her?"

Darcy nodded. "Yes, yes, she is to see everything. Nothing is off limits. I am sorry that you did not have time to prepare as you would have liked," he apologized. "And..." he paused and lowered his eyes for a moment. Mrs. Cole was adamant with her staff that proper channels were always followed. One must not overstep one's bounds, she always said. It was a firmly set rule, and he knew he had asked Sam to step out of his bounds and inform staff of news that was rightfully Mrs. Cole's or Mr. Palmer's to share. "I may have asked Sam to tell the others." He grimaced slightly at the admission.

Mrs. Cole laughed. "She is that special is she?" She gave him that smile she had always used when he had done something particularly well as a child.

"Without a doubt."

"Then we are very pleased for you, Mr. Darcy. Very pleased indeed. And, have no fear, everything will be shown to best advantage."

She lay a hand on his arm. It was not something she did very often. In fact, he could not remember the last time she had done so. It had been so long ago. "I know I overstep my bounds, but I must say how delighted I am to see that spark back in your eye. It does my old heart good to see you happy." She gave his arm a pat. "So very happy," she muttered as she hurried away.

The knocker tapped against the door, and Darcy grabbed the handle before Mr. Palmer could. "Just this once," said Darcy. "Allow me to be first to welcome her."

Mr. Palmer shook his head. "Just like your father," he said. "He always wanted to be first to greet your mother." He made a sweeping bow and then took his place next to the door.

Chapter 4

Elizabeth nervously smoothed her skirts as she waited for the door to Darcy House to open. Both her uncle Gareth's and Bingley's homes in town were grand, but neither was as grand as this. It should not have surprised her, she supposed. She had seen Pemberley. She tapped the knocker on the door a second time. After only a few moments the door opened. Her eyes grew wide in surprise before a pleased smile spread across her face, reaching her eyes and lighting them with delight.

"Mr. Darcy!" She laughed lightly. "I had not expected to see you so directly."

"You did not?" He smiled at her.

She shook her head. "It is not unwelcome, however."

He extended his hand, and when she placed hers in it, he drew her into the house. "Mrs.

Amberly, this is Mr. Palmer, who was kind enough to allow me to greet you in his place."

"Ma'am," the grey-haired man bowed slightly in greeting.

"A pleasure to meet you, Mr. Palmer."

"The pleasure is mine, ma'am." He turned to Mr. Darcy. "Miss Darcy will be expecting you in the yellow sitting room, sir."

Darcy placed Elizabeth's hand on his arm and led her to a sitting room that was bright and cheery. The morning sun streamed through the large windows, dancing across the carpet and glimmering on the tops of tables. The furniture was neatly arranged in small groupings, each with its own carpet, none of which were of the same design, yet all complemented the others.

"It is lovely," said Elizabeth, stopping just inside the door to survey the room.

"Georgiana had a hand in decorating this room. I fear I am not very skilled in arranging furnishings or choosing fabrics."

She smiled at him. "I find that hard to believe, Mr. Darcy. You are always impeccably dressed. You must have some skill."

"I have a man for that," he replied with a smile.

"And a tailor with a good eye for colour and details."

"I am sorry I was delayed. I hear I missed Mr. Darcy playing butler," Georgiana gave Elizabeth a quick hug and her brother, a wink. "Were his skills up to standard?"

Elizabeth laughed. "He has potential," she replied. "Should the need ever arise, I believe he is capable of working his way into such a position."

Darcy shook his head. "I have gone soft to allow such teasing."

"Quite right," agreed Elizabeth. "I do remember once being told that you were not to be teased."

"Miss Bingley," Darcy explained to his confused sister. "That is the only good that has come from this whole thing. I have not seen her in five years."

Elizabeth sighed. "It may have been good for you, but I can assure you it has not been for me. She married before me. She has the finest carriage, the best clothing, and the most precious children, or so she has informed me on many occasions." She moved to follow Georgiana to a grouping of chairs near the window, but Darcy caught her hand and would not allow it.

"Georgiana, you really should see the equipage in which Mrs. Amberly arrived. It is very like the one you were describing to me."

Georgiana looked at him in confusion. "I do not remember describing any carriage to you."

"Perhaps it was someone else," he said with a raised brow and a pointed look. "However, I recommend you take a look at it, so that when I remember who it was and wish to speak to you of it, you will know of what I speak."

"I would like to know of what you speak now," she said still confused.

"Look at the carriage. Please."

He could see the understanding dawn in her eyes.

"A long look?" she asked with a smile.

He nodded, and she took a place at the window with her back towards him. She prattled on about the horses and markings, as well as the driver's cap and coat, while Darcy drew Elizabeth into his embrace and kissed her. When Georgiana began commenting on how the horses were shifting from one foot to the other and flicking their heads, he reluctantly stopped and released Elizabeth from his embrace.

"I must go visit your uncle's solicitor." There was a note of regret in his voice. "I would rather send Georgiana and keep you to myself, but I cannot." He glanced at his sister and seeing that her back was still to him, he gave Elizabeth one more kiss before taking his leave.

"You will be able to see him depart from here," said Georgiana motioning for Elizabeth to join her. "We have two hours before the modiste arrives," she added as Elizabeth took a place at the window next to her.

"Arrives? We are not going to her shop?" Elizabeth asked in surprise.

"It is her preference. She is very particular, but her work is excellent." Georgiana smiled reassuringly at Elizabeth. "Mrs. Cole, the housekeeper, will join us here shortly. She wanted to accompany us on the tour in case there is anything you see that you would like to have changed, or if you have any particular questions about how things are done. Her aunt worked here before she did, so she knows everything about the house and its history, as well as about my parents, my brother and me. She is a dear woman."

Elizabeth watched as Darcy entered his carriage. It was not until it drove away that she took a seat near Georgiana. "I admit to being a bit over-whelmed by all that is happening. Not unpleasantly overwhelmed, but overwhelmed just the same." Elizabeth looked around the room. In one week, this would be her sitting room. In a week, Mr. Palmer would be her butler; Mrs. Cole, whom she had yet to meet, would be her housekeeper; and she was certain there were countless other staff who would be looking to her as their mistress. She imagined curious ladies filling the chairs in this room, and her heart began to beat a bit more rapidly.

"You will be marvelous as Mrs. Darcy," assured Georgiana.

"How can you say that with any amount of certainty? You have only just met me. It is true that it is the second meeting, but our acquaintance is of such a short duration."

Georgiana leaned toward Elizabeth. "It was not only you and my brother who were disappointed that you did not marry five years ago. Mrs. Reynolds was impressed with you the last time we met. I have heard her say over the years how she was certain my brother was going to marry you and how fine a mistress of Pemberley you would have made. She will be delighted to hear this news." Georgiana rose. "Mrs. Cole, I would like you to meet Mrs. Amberly, formerly Miss Bennet, and soon to be Mrs. Darcy."

"Miss Bennet, you say?" Mrs. Cole's eyes fluttered just a bit as a wide smile spread across her face. "A pleasure to meet you, ma'am. I have heard much about you."

"Mrs. Reynolds and Mrs. Cole correspond on a regular basis," explained Georgiana. "It helps the two houses to run most efficiently."

"Oh, Judith will be so pleased to hear you have come to us at last," said Mrs. Cole, dabbing at her eyes with her handkerchief. It took her a moment to recollect herself and regain her professional demeanor. "As you can see," she began with a wave of her hand, "this is the yellow sitting room. Callers are entertained here, and Miss Darcy finds it a particularly good room for doing sewing as the windows are so large and allow in so much light." She paused for a moment to look at Elizabeth, her excitement bubbling up once again. "Oh, I am so delighted. If you follow me, I will acquaint you with your new home."

Elizabeth followed the pleasant lady from the room and around the house, trying to remember all the information she was being told and trying not to giggle at the pride with which Mrs. Cole introduced her to the staff, occasionally mentioning that this was the lady Mrs. Reynolds had mentioned and then apologizing for having spoken of it. So the day went until the modiste arrived. Then, as she stood in the mistress's chamber, Elizabeth was measured and asked to choose patterns and fabrics. By the time the modiste had left, she was feeling quite exhausted.

"You will stay for dinner, will you not?" Georgiana asked as she and Elizabeth settled into the chairs where they had started their day.

Elizabeth shook her head. "I cannot. Mrs. Amberly has invited my aunt and uncle Gardiner to dine with us tonight."

Georgiana sighed with disappointment. "You will stay until my brother returns?"

Elizabeth smiled sheepishly. "I would not think of leaving until after that."

Georgiana clapped her hands. "Good. Then we shall have tea." She rose and gave instructions to a footman in the hall. She and Elizabeth were just settling into a discussion of music when both the tea and Lady Matlock arrived. Georgiana sighed quietly as the lady was announced.

"I was not receiving callers today, my lady," said Georgiana as she rose to greet her aunt with a kiss placed quickly on her cheek.

"Yes, Palmer mentioned that, but as I told him, I am not a caller. I am your aunt." She took Georgiana by the shoulders and turned her in a circle. "You are looking well. When shall we hear of a marriage proposal?" She raised an eyebrow as she looked at Elizabeth. "I thought you were not home to callers," she chided Georgiana.

"Would you care for tea, Aunt Edith?" Georgiana moved to begin pouring. "We have some of those almond cakes which you so like."

Lady Matlock took a seat and indicated that she would indeed have tea, but her eyes never left Elizabeth.

Elizabeth, a swirling sense of unease growing in her stomach, remained standing, unsure as to whether she should sit until she had been introduced.

"Mrs. Amberly is not a caller, my lady," Georgiana finally began the introductions. "She is an old friend. Mrs. Amberly, my aunt, Lady Matlock."

Elizabeth dipped a proper curtsey and offered her greeting before returning to her seat.

Lady Matlock took a small sip of her tea and gave Georgiana a small nod of approval. "Amberly?" She peered at Elizabeth. "A relation of Mr. Gareth Amberly?" She asked the question, but her tone spoke of her already knowing the information.

"My uncle through marriage, my lady."

Lady Matlock's left brow arched. "Ah, you are Jack's widow." Her tone once again told of no surprise at this information. "Your sister is Mrs. Charles Bingley, is she not?"

"I am, and she is, my lady."

Lady Matlock turned slightly toward Georgiana. "Your brother used to be friends with Mr. Bingley, did he not?"

Georgiana smiled tightly and nodded her agreement.

"Lord Matlock was not unhappy to see that relationship end." She looked pointedly at Elizabeth. "Connections to trade and all that, surely you understand."

Elizabeth sucked in a breath. She wished to defend Bingley for Jane's sake, but how could she tout him as a fine gentleman when her thoughts of him were currently less than charitable?

"It was an unfortunate parting of ways," said Georgiana.

Lady Matlock seemed to ignore the comment, though Elizabeth did not miss the slight rise of an eyebrow. "I heard your brother made a bit of a scene last night." She took a sip of her tea. "Several scenes to be precise." She shook her head. "Calling on the archbishop at such an hour." She clucked her tongue.

Elizabeth's cheeks grew warm.

"We expect him to return soon," said Georgiana. "You may wish to ask him about whatever actions it is which have you concerned."

"Oh, is he not home?"

Peer or not, the woman's pretense of ignorance was beginning to grate on Elizabeth. It reminded her far too much of Miss Bingley. "He is visiting my uncle's solicitor," said Elizabeth, placing her half empty tea cup on a side table. "But, I am quite certain you will not find that a surprise."

Lady Matlock fumbled with her cup for only a

moment before regaining her composure. "He will have to return and undo whatever he has done." She levelled a firm stare at Elizabeth and shook her head. "You are quite unacceptable," she added.

"Perhaps to you, my lady, but not to Mr. Darcy." Elizabeth's eyes did not waver from Lady Matlock's. "You shall, unless Mr. Darcy prohibits it, be invited to family gatherings, christenings, Georgiana's wedding breakfast, Christmas, and the like. However, I will understand if you wish not to accept the invitations, and I will not censure you for it. Do not render evil for evil and all that, of course, you understand." She pulled her spine as straight as she could and squared her shoulders. "But please know that I will not release Mr. Darcy from his promise to marry me, for I shall not live another moment without him."

Lady Matlock's eyes narrowed. "You are not of his sphere."

"Is he not a gentleman?" Elizabeth asked with feigned surprise. "I had imagined him to be so."

Again, Lady Matlock fumbled with her cup before giving a shrug. "Very well, he is a gentleman, and your father was also a gentleman, even if he was tainted by trade. You are not altogether from separate spheres, though his relations are of the peerage."

"Of that I am aware, my lady," said Elizabeth.

Lady Matlock tilted her head slightly and pursed her lips. "You will not give him up?"

"Not until I draw my final breath, my lady."

Lady Matlock's eyes narrowed again, and she drank her tea as if deep in thought. Then she set the tea aside and rose, causing Georgiana and Elizabeth to rise as well out of courtesy. "You are stubborn enough to be a Darcy," she stated. "Do not expect an invitation to Matlock House."

"That will save her the awkwardness of refusing it," Darcy growled from the door.

Lady Matlock's eyes widened slightly before she turned to greet her nephew.

He held up a hand to keep her from speaking. "The time has come for you to leave." He shook his head as she once again began to speak. "It is better if we part without words, for I fear mine would be far from kind."

She gave him a nod and moved toward the door.

"Lady Matlock," he called after her, causing her to turn towards him. "Do tell my uncle of this and inform him that nothing shall move me from my position. And while you are at it, you might remind him that Amberly is not without connections, my lady. He is a graduate of Oxford and a Tory, is he not?" Darcy looked to Elizabeth to answer.

"Indeed, and very interested in the workings of government," she replied, earning a truly beautiful smile from Mr. Darcy.

"Yes, remind my uncle of that also," he said without looking at his aunt for he was unwilling to take his eyes from his Elizabeth. He waited until he heard the door to Darcy House close. "You are well?" he asked.

"I am."

"And you, Georgiana?" He asked turning to his sister, who smiled and nodded.

"We should finish our tea," said Georgiana returning to her seat and taking up her cup. "Elizabeth was brilliant." She took a small sip of tea. "Aunt Edith rattled her cup twice."

"Twice?" Darcy repeated in surprise. "Not even Lady Catherine has rattled Lady Matlock more than once in a sitting." Admiration coloured his tone.

Elizabeth chuckled. "You approve of disquieting your relations?"

"Only the impossible ones," he said steering her by her elbow to a settee so that he might sit with her. "I was quite enchanted with how you unsettled Lady Catherine."

"No!" said Georgiana. "Lady Catherine, too?" Her eyes shone with amusement. "You must tell me the tale."

And so with Elizabeth's hand in his, he did.

Chapter 5

Elizabeth was seated at her dressing table when the door to the bedroom flew open.

"What do you mean you are marrying Mr. Darcy?" Jane held the note Elizabeth had sent in her right hand and waved it slightly to draw her sister's attention to it. "You have not seen him in five years, and at your first re-acquaintance you agree to marry him?" She tossed the letter on Elizabeth's table and folded her arms across her chest. "When Jack died, you said you would never marry again, and yet you are betrothed to the first man you are introduced to at a ball?" Her tone was accusing and, for Jane, she spoke loudly.

Elizabeth sighed. Of course, Jane did not understand. Elizabeth had never spoken of Mr. Darcy after Bingley returned without him. She rose, dismissed her maid, and went to sit on the bed, motioning for Jane to join her.

"How could you accept him?" Though Jane's voice had quieted, her tone was no less accusing.

Elizabeth grasped Jane's hands, trying to calm not only Jane but also herself. Admitting she had kept a secret from her dearly loved sister was not an easy task. For all their lives, they had shared nearly everything. "I know it appears sudden, but I assure you it is not." She looked steadfastly at their joined hands. "I love him," she admitted, daring only to peek up at her sister. Her heart thumped loudly in her chest as it always did when Jane was distraught. "I have loved him nearly as long as you have loved Charles." She released one of Jane's hands and brushed a tear from the corner of her eye.

Jane cupped her sister's cheek with her free hand.

Elizabeth gave her a small smile of thanks at the comforting gesture. Even when distraught, Jane found it nearly impossible to refrain from giving comfort.

"But what of his interference with Charles and me? You were so angry with him."

Elizabeth nodded slowly. "I was, and while I cannot approve of his actions in doing so, I do understand his reasons. He has repented of any harm he may have caused, and I have forgiven him long ago." She covered Jane's hand, which was still on her cheek, with her own. "My dear sister," her voice was gentle, "how did your husband learn of Mr. Darcy's interference?"

Jane blinked apparently unsure of why Elizabeth would ask such a question. "Mr. Darcy told him of it."

Elizabeth nodded and rose from the bed. It was too difficult to stay seated. The topic was not an easy one of which to speak. Her stomach twisted and knotted. Her hands clasped each other tightly and then relaxed before repeating the same process. "Mr. Darcy did not have to tell Charles of it. He could have encouraged Charles simply to return to Netherfield and renew his acquaintance with you without ever divulging his part in your separation." She stood by the window and peeked over her shoulder at her sister, who was watching her with furrowed brows. "Mr. Darcy told Charles because of me."

"I do not understand." Jane shook her head in confusion.

Elizabeth drew a deep breath and released it. Why now, after finally being happily reunited with Darcy, must her heart still ache so? She glanced over her shoulder once again at her sister and found her answer. The telling of the tale brought the danger of injuring her sister. The knot in her stomach twisted more tightly, causing her to wrap her arms around her middle.

"You are not well." Jane was at her side in an instant. "Let me call your maid again, and we can get you into bed." She lay her hand on her sister's cheek and then forehead. "You do not feel feverish."

"I am not ill," said Elizabeth. "I refused him. Five years ago, I refused Mr. Darcy because of what Wickham had told me and because he had caused you pain." Tears slid silently down her cheeks.

Jane, with a concerned, yet puzzled, look on her face, held Elizabeth by her shoulders, and once once again placed a hand on her sister's cheek.

"Mr. Darcy separated you and Charles," Elizabeth continued, "because he was afraid Charles

was more attached to you than you were to him."
She looked at the floor. "He was sorry when he
learned how you had been injured. I believe he
wished to make amends by telling Charles of his
part."

Jane drew Elizabeth into an embrace. "I am still
unsure how this has led to your acceptance, but
you are trembling. Please, come, if you will not
allow me to assist you into bed, you must sit with
me."

Elizabeth allowed her sister to lead her to the
bed where they sat, Jane with her arms around her
sister and Elizabeth with her head on Jane's shoulder. As painful as it was to speak of any of this,
there was also a comfort in no longer carrying the
secret alone. They sat quietly for a moment before
Elizabeth continued. "I came to understand him
after my refusal and grew to love him as I began
to see our interactions in a different light. I both
hoped for and feared an opportunity to see him
again. So, when we met again in Derbyshire before
Lydia's marriage, I was pleased that he welcomed
Aunt and Uncle and me. And after some time
spent in his company, I was hopeful that he would
renew his addresses."

"But he did not." Jane stroked Elizabeth's hair back from her face.

"He was prevented," Elizabeth whispered.

"By what happened with Lydia?" asked Jane.

Elizabeth shook her head. "That is what I thought, but it is not true."

"Then by what?" Jane leaned back to look at Elizabeth.

"I do not wish to hurt you," Elizabeth drew and released a shuddering breath, attempting to keep her emotions from overwhelming her. She could not bear to be the one to see her sister disappointed in Charles.

"You must tell me," Jane demanded.

"I cannot."

"You must!"

Elizabeth shook her head and pulling away from her sister, buried her face in her hands. "I am sorry."

Jane sighed in frustration. "What would have prevented Mr. Darcy from returning to Hertford-shire to call on you? I know Charles was angry, so Mr. Darcy might not have been welcomed at Netherfield, but there is an inn."

Elizabeth heard Jane's gasp and knew that her sister had discovered the truth of what happened.

Jane lifted Elizabeth's face to look at her. "Was it Charles' anger?"

Elizabeth bit her lip and nodded as tears streamed down her cheeks. "I am sorry," she whispered again.

Jane's eyes began to widen as she grasped what had happened. "Charles would not allow it?"

Elizabeth nodded again. "Mr. Darcy hoped he would relent. He sent Charles letters begging his forgiveness, but to no avail." A sob shook her.

Jane pulled her close. "Charles did this?" There was a sharpness to her tone. "Five years," she gasped. "Oh, my dear, dear sister, how you must have suffered." She rubbed Elizabeth's back as they sat silently, save for a few sniffles. "But what of Jack?" Jane finally asked when Elizabeth's tears had stopped. "Surely you were happy with Jack?"

"I was. He was good to me, and I cared for him."

"Did you love him?" Jane's question was no more than a whisper.

"We loved each other in a way, but I did not,

could not, love him completely. I thought I might be able to eventually, but I know now that it was a vain hope. My heart was irrevocably gone. I do not regret my marriage, but I do regret not being able to give myself to Jack completely." She pulled back from her sister's shoulder and looked at her. "It is why I said I would never marry another after Jack died. I knew I would never be able to give my whole heart to any man unless..." She shrugged.

Jane's eyes were filled with tears. "Unless it was Mr. Darcy." She pulled Elizabeth back into her embrace and squeezed her tightly. "Oh, my dear, dear sister, you have been so wronged!"

Elizabeth could hear the fury that bubbled beneath her sister's words. She could feel the stiffening of Jane's posture.

"It has been made right," Elizabeth said in hopes of calming Jane's anger. Jane was rarely angry, but when she was, it was a determined anger that would only be placated when whatever wrong had been committed had been put to right.

"No." Jane shook her head firmly. "It has not. There is still my husband's part." She pulled back and looked at her sister. "Might I borrow a pen and paper?"

Elizabeth looked at her with trepidation. "If I might know why they are needed."

"I must make arrangements for a stay at our aunt and uncle Gardiners."

"Oh, Jane, you mustn't," Elizabeth cried. "I could not bear to be the cause of distress between you and Charles."

Jane raised an eyebrow. There was a determined line to her jaw. "Mr. Bingley is the cause." She shook her head. "I do not know why I did not inquire more about your melancholy mood. What pain I might have saved you if I had!" She stood. "My husband must feel a portion."

"Jane, please,"' begged Elizabeth, although she knew it was to no avail. Jane possessed a sweet temperament, but she was not without her portion of Bennet stubbornness, especially when someone had been ill-used.

Jane cupped Elizabeth's face in her hands and smiled at her. "It shall not be for a long duration, but he must have what he loves ripped from him as you have had done to you. What did Papa always say? An illustration is a far better teacher than a lecture?"

"But, Jane —."

"No. It must be."

There was a finality to the tone of Jane's voice, and Elizabeth knew that no amount of pleading would sway her. She sighed. "Very well. I shall get you paper and pen."

Jane patted Elizabeth's cheek and smiled. "Ah, now there is a good girl."

"I am not convinced of my goodness in this," replied Elizabeth.

Jane pulled her sister from the bed and wrapped her once more in her arms. "All will be well in time. I will not let it be otherwise," she promised.

~*~*~*~

Three letters had been written — one to Charles, one to Aunt Gardiner, and a third to Jane's housekeeper. Jane was determined that she would not return to her house even to gather her things until five days — one for each year of Elizabeth's suffering — had passed. So the children, as well as all the things necessary for a stay of five days, were delivered to Jane at Grace Church Street.

Elizabeth had received a note that evening saying all was well with Jane and the children and promising to call when they were settled. And then, for the next two days, Elizabeth heard nothing from her sister. Naturally, she worried and fretted as one would when a constant correspondent and dear sister leaves to create a stir in her home on your behalf. And so, after fidgeting about, unable to focus on any particular activity for the whole of the morning on the second day, Elizabeth was done with waiting and was just sitting to write a note to Jane when there was a gentle tapping at her sitting room door, and Georgiana entered.

"Would you like to go for a drive with me and then return to Darcy House for tea?" Georgiana asked as she took a seat near Elizabeth. "My brother paces in front of the windows incessantly." She shook her head. "He cannot seem to calm himself. He gets this way before an anticipated event. He worries." She smiled at Elizabeth. "I know he will continue his pacing until you are married, but he relaxes for a while after you have called." She sighed. "He seems worse today."

Elizabeth placed her pen back in its holder. "I am worried myself."

"About the wedding?" Georgiana's eyes grew wide.

"Oh, not about marrying your brother," Elizabeth assured her. "That, I am quite happy to do."

Georgiana chuckled.

"I still have not heard from my sister," said Elizabeth. "She has neither called nor written, — and it is very unlike her. If she would but write, I might be, at least, somewhat at ease."

"A drive might be distracting."

Elizabeth smiled at the hopeful tone in Georgiana's voice. "It might be at that. I will get my things." She rose from her desk to go fetch her bonnet when her maid entered with a letter.

"Perhaps I worried for nothing," Elizabeth said as she broke the seal and sat next to Georgiana. Then ,holding the missive so that they both might see it, Elizabeth began reading.

> *Dearest Lizzy,*
>
> *I must beg your forgiveness for my delay in writing to you. Indeed, as you know, I had hoped to call in person, but settling the children into their new surroundings has been more of a chore than I had anticipated. They are good but excited to be visiting their cousins. I am very grateful to have*

*the help of the Misses Gardiner. They are much
like their mother, you know, and excellent with children.*

*Charles has called twice and written as well.
I have refused to see him or even read his letters.
I sent them back to him this morning. I know it
is cruel, but he was no less cruel to you and Mr.
Darcy. I must admit that my curiosity nearly con-
sumes me, and I am uncertain that I can refrain
from reading the next letter, should there be one, for
I would dearly love to hear his reply to my departure. However, I remain determined to have no
contact with him for five days complete. Only then,
shall I reply. It is but a small measure of pain com-
pared to what you have endured.*

*I trust you are well. I shall endeavour to call
tomorrow.*

Yours ever,

Jane

Elizabeth blew out a breath. "While I understand why she is doing it, and I appreciate her support, I cannot help feeling guilty."

Georgiana patted Elizabeth's arm reassuringly.
"It is not your fault that Mr. Bingley acted as he
did, and it is not as if you forced your sister to

respond to the news as she did." She smiled at Elizabeth. "I have learned that you can only be responsible for your own actions." She stood. "Now, for that drive. Would it inconvenience your aunt if we were to visit?"

Elizabeth bit her lip and looked at the letter in her hand. "She would not be troubled by it; however, if Mr. Bingley were to arrive while we were there..." She turned the letter over in her hand.

Georgiana sat back down. "Write her a note. Our drive will wait."

Chapter 6

Darcy rose to greet the man who had come to call on him. "Bingley," he said with a nod of his head.

"Darcy." There was a noticeable gruffness to Bingley's tone, and he held his hat in his hand as if the meeting were to be of a very brief duration. He walked to Darcy's desk and tossed two envelopes down on it.

Darcy picked them up and turned them over. "Why are you delivering mail to me that is addressed to your wife?"

"I told you to stay away from my family," said Bingley.

"And I have," said Darcy, placing the letters back on the desk and pushing them toward Bingley.

"These," Bingley picked up the letters and waved them in front of Darcy, "were returned to me unopened, and my sweet wife has moved to her aunt's home and refuses to see me because of you." He rested his fists on the desk and leaned toward his friend. "You were supposed to stay away from my family," he repeated through clenched teeth.

Darcy shook his head and turned away to rummage in a drawer behind him. "How long has she been gone?"

"What difference does that make?" asked Bingley. "She is gone."

Darcy placed a stack of envelopes on his desk. "How long?" He leveled a glare at Bingley.

"Two days."

"And she has returned two letters?"

"As you can see," said Bingley in exasperation, waving the letters once again.

Darcy tapped the stack of letters in front of him. "How many letters do you think are in this packet?" He began to untie the string that held the bundle together.

Bingley shook his head. "I could not say."

Darcy smiled. He found the confusion on Bingley's face strangely pleasing. He had wondered how he might react to seeing Bingley again. He had imagined various scenarios of angry confrontation

— raised voices, strong language, fists, and even swords. However, now, with the man in front of him, Darcy felt a calm deep within his spirit mingled with a sadness that left him feeling as if he should be retiring for the night. He felt no need to assault the man as he had imagined he might. Instead, he longed to state his case, to be heard at last. And maybe, just maybe, to have Bingley understand all that had transpired.

"There are twenty," Darcy said as he spread them out on the desk. "All addressed to you. None opened." He chose the letter from the bottom of the pile. It was one which he knew contained the whole of his responsibility in separating Bingley and Jane as well as his plea to see Elizabeth. This was what he hoped Bingley would hear. How many times had he written of these things? He had tried to explain it to Bingley the dreadful day of his confession; however, his pleas, like these letters, had fallen on ears unwilling to hear. "Do you have any idea what is contained within this?" He broke the seal. "I suspect it is very much the same as what you have written to your wife — a plea for forgiveness, a begging that things might be restored." He unfolded the letter and allowed his eyes to scan it.

The pain of each word pricking again in his heart. "Five years," he said softly, "is much longer than two days." He dropped the letter on the desk. "I hope you are more successful than I."

Darcy took a seat and motioned for Bingley to take one as well, which he did after a moment's hesitation. "I did as you asked. I have not contacted you or any member of your family for five years."

"But you are engaged to Elizabeth!"

Darcy nodded. "Her uncle brought her to me. I did not seek her out."

"You should have walked away," muttered Bingley.

"As you would walk away from your wife?" asked Darcy, his tone less than pleasant.

"I do not follow," said Bingley. "Why would I walk away from my wife? I love her."

"And yet, you would ask me to walk away from the woman I love." Darcy smiled wryly and picked up the opened letter. "A fact you would have known had you listened to me five years ago or bothered to read just one of these letters." He closed his eyes and shook his head. "I walked away from Elizabeth for five years, Bingley. Five years!

And do you know why? Because you asked me to do so. I have never been a bigger fool. Never!"

"Loved her?" Bingley scoffed. "How does a man walk away from the woman he loves because of the words of a friend? It cannot be a very strong attachment if he does."

Darcy pushed away from his desk. His jaw clenched in frustration. Any peace he had felt before had vanished in the face of Bingley's unwillingness to listen. "You left Netherfield with very little encouragement to do so." He could not keep the anger out of his voice. "You chose to leave. No one forced you, and yet, you treat me as if I had abducted Miss Bennet and locked her away in a tower so that you could not reach her." He stood. "Your sister did far more to discourage the match than I ever did. I told you that I did not think Miss Bennet partial to you. Caroline refused to see her when in town and sent her a letter hinting that you were to marry Georgiana — Georgiana!" He threw his hands in the air. "Did you banish your sister, or am I the only one to have suffered for your foolishness?" He turned away from his friend and then hastily turned back. "No. No, I did not suffer alone. Elizabeth has suffered as well." He pushed the open letter toward Bingley. "Read it. I will hear no more from you until you have heard the whole sorry business." With that, he stalked to the door.

"Campbell," he called down the hall, then waited until the man joined him. "This man is not to be admitted to this house again without the letter I have just given him in his possession." He turned to Bingley. "Your wife, however, will always be welcomed, for I could not bear to separate Elizabeth from her sister." He gave the hem of his jacket a tug. "I will be in the yellow sitting room if either of you need me."

"Mrs. Amberly has just arrived, sir," said the butler.

Darcy closed his eyes for a moment before turning back toward Bingley. "Mrs. Amberly," he said emphasizing the title. "Miss Bennet was still Miss Bennet when you returned to Netherfield. Imagine if she had not been." He gave a nod to his butler and left the room.

"She's a lovely lady. Mrs. Amberly is. Thought she was going to be our mistress years ago, but it is set right now."

Darcy chuckled when he heard it and stopped to wait for Mr. Campbell to join him.

"I know it is not proper, sir," Campbell explained as he reached his employer, "but he needed to know."

Darcy clapped the man on the shoulder. "I appreciate your loyalty, Campbell. It was well done. Now, will I find Mrs. Amberly in the sitting room?"

"I assume so, sir. She and Miss Darcy were startled by the commotion, and I dared not tarry in heeding your call."

"My apologies, Campbell," muttered Darcy. Yelling and bellowing were not things that Darcy did so he could imagine how doing so might have unnerved his faithful servant.

"No, need to apologize, sir. I assume there was just cause" replied Campbell with a nod.

"While that is true, Campbell, I should not have raised my voice to you."

"This is one time, sir," Campbell looked back toward the door to Darcy's study, "that yelling is not only allowed but expected." He turned back to his employer and with a smile very unlike a butler and more like an older, wiser friend, he said, "There is a lady awaiting you, sir."

Darcy could not help the smile that formed on his lips. She was waiting for him. His Elizabeth was waiting for him. He hurried down the hall and to the sitting room.

"Are things well?" asked Georgiana as he entered.

He gave her a small smile. "They will be if there is a carriage at which you can look."

Georgiana shook her head and rolled her eyes at her brother. "I believe I might be able to find one."

He winked at her and gathered Elizabeth, who stood next to Georgiana, into his arms and held her firmly against his chest.

"What has happened?" Elizabeth asked. She could hear his heart's rapid beat with her ear pressed against him as it was.

He kissed the top of her head. "I will tell you in a moment."

She rubbed small circles on his back where her arms wrapped around his middle. She wanted to ask him again about whatever it was that was disturbing him, but instead, she listened to his heart as it gradually returned to a steady, regular beat.

Georgiana made a shuffling noise from where she stood by the window, and Elizabeth attempted to pull away from Darcy.

"Just one more carriage, Georgiana," Darcy said.

The comment was met with a sigh, and Elizabeth tried again to pull away.

Darcy smiled down at her, his eyes holding hers for a moment and then lowering to her lips and returning to her eyes.

She returned his smile with a welcoming one of her own.

A few delightful moments later, Georgiana coughed.

Darcy released Elizabeth from his embrace and catching her hand, led her to a settee where Georgiana joined them.

"Bingley is here," he said as Georgiana was just taking her seat. "He is furious that Jane had gone to the Gardiners and blames me." He wrapped Elizabeth's small hand inside his large ones. "He is still unwilling to listen, so I left him with a letter — one of the ones I wrote him five years ago."

"You kept them?" Elizabeth's eyes were filled with surprise and a small amount of sorrow. "Such painful things to keep."

Darcy nodded. Those letters had been a constant torment to him for months as, at first, one and then another was returned unopened. He had tried to burn them on several occasions, but he could not. He was not entirely sure why he had felt compelled to keep them, but he had.

"Twenty!" Bingley said from the door, a stack of opened letters in each hand. "All are nearly the same." He took a step into the room but stopped. "May I enter?"

Darcy motioned for him to join them.

Bingley blinked, and his lips twitched as if trying to contain his emotions. "They vary only in the tone of desperation," he said softly. His hands, filled with papers, hung at his side, and his gaze dropped to the floor. "I do not know what to say other than I was wrong. I would beg your forgiveness, but I am certain I do not deserve it."

"You do not, but is forgiveness ever deserved?" asked Darcy. "Or is it a gift bestowed, and not easily so, by the one wronged?"

"The harm I caused," said Bingley looking first

at the letters in his hand and then at Darcy and, finally, Elizabeth. "It is so great."

"It is," agreed Elizabeth. She stood and reached for the letters Bingley held. "Please?" she said when he did not seem willing to give them to her. "Be seated," she added as he relinquished the papers.

Returning to her seat, Elizabeth smoothed the papers on her lap. The fine, close writing begged to be read, but she refrained from reading more than a phrase or two; however, it was enough of a glimpse into the pain of the man who wrote them. She looked up from the letters and into Bingley's eyes, which glistened with unshed tears. "Jane and the children are settling in well at the Gardiners. The children are excited to see their cousins." She drew a deep breath. "I tried not to let her know of your part in my separation from Mr. Darcy, for I did not wish to cause you pain by causing strife between you and Jane." She saw him bite his lip, which trembled slightly as his eyes blinked away the tears that gathered at their rims.

Elizabeth lowered her gaze to the letters. "Before we can move forward, as we must, for we are family, it is necessary that you hear from me."

Her hands smoothed over the papers on her lap once again before she began telling her tale of growing to love Darcy. She told of her refusal of his first offer of marriage and the letter Darcy had written to her in response. She told of her time of contemplation and re-evaluation of the man she thought she knew. She told of how she began to be uncertain she knew him at all, only to discover that it was not true. She knew him well. He was a man to be esteemed, a man who was her best match in every possible way. She continued her tale with her hope at Pemberley and how it had been crushed by Lydia's elopement and Darcy's failure to return with Bingley. "I mourned for what could have been. I knew not why he had abandoned you or me, but I believed it to be because of Lydia. Eventually, I came to a place where I had to accept that my first and greatest love was gone, and so I began my friendship with Jack."

Bingley grabbed her hands, which were once again smoothing the letters. "Tell me no more," he pleaded. "I cannot fathom having returned to Hertfordshire and finding Jane with another." At this, a tear pushed through the blinking of eyelashes and slid down his cheek. "If Jack had lived..." his voice trailed off.

"I would have continued my friendship with him and never ventured to London for a season, and I would be none the wiser about any of this. I would remain as I was, content but not completely happy. Loving, but not fully."

"Please, no more," Bingley begged as other tears chased the first one down his cheek. "Tell Jane I will await her return but understand if it is not soon."

Elizabeth shook her head. "You must not retreat. There are twenty letters on my lap, and I dare say there would be hundreds more if you had not told Mr. Darcy to desist." She leaned toward Bingley, her hands still grasped in his. "Write constantly. Call every day. Only stop when she tells you to stop and not a moment before. And then hope, even when the world looks bleak and the way seems impossible because, sometimes, the impossible fades into the greatest joy of your life." She squeezed his hands tightly. "Promise me that you will go home and write to Jane and that in the morning you will do so again."

He nodded. "I do not deserve your kindness."

She looked at Darcy and then back at Bingley. "Perhaps you do not, but does anyone ever deserve kindness, or is it a gift bestowed by the giver?" She arched a brow in question and then smiled impertinently.

Bingley chuckled despite his tears.

"Go home," Elizabeth said once again. "Write to my sister and in three day's time, join us here for our wedding."

Bingley looked to Darcy. "I would be welcomed?"

Darcy took the pile of letters from Elizabeth's lap and shuffled through them. "If you have this," he said handing the letter to Bingley. "I did, after all, instruct Campbell that he was not to admit you without it."

Taking the letter, Bingley folded it and placed it in his pocket.

"I cannot say how we will move on from here, but it shall not be done separately." Darcy stood and extended his hand to Bingley. "I once told you that my good opinion once lost was lost forever; however, that is not true. Although you may have lost it for a time, that does not mean it cannot be restored with time and effort."

Bingley gripped Darcy's hand tightly and gave it a firm shake. "Thank you. I shall endeavor to deserve it."

Darcy stood looking at the door after Bingley had left. His musings about what had transpired were halted, however, when Elizabeth wound her arm around his.

"You were very forgiving," she said. "Very unlike a gentleman with an implacable temper." She favored him with a teasing smile.

He chuckled. "As were you."

"What other option was there?"

"None. I would not see you separated from your sister," he looked down at her, "and I would be lying if I said I had not missed him. He was much like a brother."

"A younger, more foolish one." Georgiana giggled at the surprised looks on Elizabeth and Darcy's faces. "You had forgotten I was here," she said as she rose from her seat. "I am happy for both of you." She looked toward the window and then back at her brother with a twinkle in her eye. "I do not relish the thought of admiring any more carriages, so perhaps I shall go to my room and conduct a search of several minutes for something that I might show Elizabeth?"

"A very good idea," replied Darcy. "Will you play for us when you return?"

She grinned widely. "When I return with very heavy footsteps, I shall play for you if you promise to behave while I do so."

Darcy shook his head. "I make no promises." He waved his hand toward the door in a sweeping motion. "Now be off so I might kiss Elizabeth."

Georgiana giggled and scooted toward the door.

"And close the door," he added.

"I do hope you remember my compliance when my turn comes," she said as she reached the door.

"If you have been separated from him for five years, I shall consider it." The words bounced back to him from the inside surface of the door. "She will claim she heard only half of it — the half she wishes." He wrapped his arms around Elizabeth. "If Mr. Murrish would just get on with it, she might soon be happily settled." A hand placed softly on his cheek drew his attention back to the woman in his arms.

"If Mr. Darcy would just get on with it," Elizabeth suggested, her thumb caressing the lightly shadowed skin of his jaw.

And he did.

Chapter 7

Jane spun her sister around in a circle. "Beautiful," she sighed as she pulled Elizabeth into a gentle embrace, taking care not to crush one bit of the lovely white muslin gown her sister wore. She held Elizabeth at arm's length and then, after studying her sister for a moment longer, straightened the silk sash on Elizabeth's dress and fluffed the sleeves. "Are you happy?"

Elizabeth nodded, a smile splitting her face. "I have never been more so."

"I remember another day like this when I asked you the same question," said Jane with a raised brow.

Elizabeth remembered that day, too. Her answer on that day had been, "I believe I am." It had been honest enough to not prick her conscience and delivered with enough of a smile to be acceptable to her sister after a moment of scrutiny. A moment very similar to the one she faced now as Jane tilted her head and studied her with narrowed eyes.

"I find your answer today to be much more satisfactory." Jane gave Elizabeth another hug and then, though they did not need it, she straightened Elizabeth's sash and sleeves again. "I worried about you." She plucked at one of the small yellow flowers that adorned the sleeve of Elizabeth's gown. "You were not so happy as I had been, and I could not discern the reason. If I had but inquired more..."

Elizabeth shook her head to stop her sister from saying anything further. She and Jane had canvassed this subject twice already. Twice Elizabeth had assured her sister that she had been content. Jane's gaze had dropped to the floor, so Elizabeth lifted her sister's chin. "Are you happy still?" she asked.

"I will be." Jane had not yet returned to her home, nor had she spoken to or seen her husband.

She fidgeted again with Elizabeth's dress. "I do not know what I will do when I see him," she admitted.

Elizabeth stilled Jane's hands. "You will be proper and caring. You always are." Elizabeth's smile and words were gentle. "Will you return to your home?" Until last evening, when Elizabeth had last seen her, Jane had been uncertain of the best path to reconciliation. She was torn between staying at the Gardiners until things were resolved or returning home.

"We have much to discuss." Her eyes were fixed on where her hands were joined with her sisters.

"You do," agreed Elizabeth, "but do not spend another day separated from him, Jane. Aunt and Uncle will gladly keep the children."

Jane sighed. "I know. I do miss him." She lifted her eyes to Elizabeth's. "He is truly penitent?"

It was a question Elizabeth had answered at least once on each of the last two days. "He is." Elizabeth dropped her sister's hands and pulled a box out of her trunk, which was the last of her things still needing to be delivered to Darcy House. From the box, she took five letters. "I told him to write you every day, once in the morning and once in the evening and to never give up on you until you told him to do so." She held the letters out to her sister. "He did."

Jane took the letters, a puzzled expression on her face. "He gave them to you?"

Elizabeth nodded. "I was to decide if you would ever be given them, just as he decided that Mr. Darcy's letters would never be known to me. He is very conscience-stricken." She snatched the letters back from Jane. "Oh, do not open them!" she cried. "One should not attend a wedding with a swollen red nose."

Jane giggled. "But I am so curious."

Elizabeth could well imagine that she was. "He loves you, Jane. He has made his apologies to all those he has wronged — save you." Once again, she held the letters out to her sister. "You may read them after you have completed your responsibilities of standing up with me." She raised a brow and gave her sister a stern look. "Not a tear until then."

"Not even happy ones?" Jane asked as she dabbed the corner of one eye with her handkerchief.

"A few might be acceptable," conceded Elizabeth, linking arms with her sister and exiting the room.

"Who is standing up with Mr. Darcy?" Jane asked as they descended the stairs to where Mr. Amberly waited.

"Charles is," said Elizabeth. She continued speaking over the sound of Jane's gasp. "Mr. Darcy wished to show you as clearly as he could that your husband has been forgiven, and since Uncle Gareth is already filling Papa's role, he could not do both." She smiled at her uncle. "Although, we are both very grateful to him for his scheming in bringing us together."

"It was a pleasure." He offered her his arm. "The carriage awaits, my ladies." He bowed slightly. "Franklin, Mrs. Amberly's trunk is to be delivered straight away," he reminded his butler. "It is the last time I shall call you that, my dear."

Elizabeth squeezed his arm more tightly.

"Jack made me promise to see you happy," Mr. Amberly said as they exited the house, "and I vowed to see you even more happy than you had been with him." He smiled at her and patted her hand. "Oh, I knew you were as happy as you could be with him, and I am so grateful to have had you added to my family. It is the best thing that has happened to Stella and me since taking Jack in after his parents died. The very best thing." He made sure she was settled into the carriage before turning to assist Jane and then his wife. "I might be allowing you to marry Mr. Darcy, but you will remain a part of my family." His tone was unusually serious for a typically very merry gentleman.

"I would have it no other way," assured Elizabeth. "You have been very good to me, and I am grateful more than words can ever tell. But it is more than that, and you know it." She smiled at him and then sighed. "I fear we may find ourselves in need of family since I do not believe Lord and Lady Matlock or Lady Catherine will be receiving us in their homes or calling on us at ours."

Mr. Amberly climbed in and settled in next to his wife, a knowing smile on his face. "Oh, Lord Matlock will accept you."

Elizabeth looked at him in surprise.

He shrugged. "He wishes my support, and if I have to force him to like you, I will." His eyes twinkled. "For I know once he has made your acquaintance, he shall be hard pressed not to be charmed."

He nodded to the footman that he was ready, and the door was closed and latched.

Not more than half an hour later, Elizabeth stood at the far end of the yellow drawing room in front of a large set of doors which opened out onto a small terrace. Here, with a few friends and family gathered around, she placed her hand in Darcy's and pledged herself to him.

Jane smiled throughout the entire ceremony and much of the breakfast which followed, though she did dab at her eyes several times.

Bingley had arrived that morning with not only the letter Darcy had required he keep to gain admittance but with an additional five copies of it, perfectly folded and bundled together.

It was, Darcy had told Elizabeth, no trifling gesture, for Bingley had never enjoyed writing letters and had always written them most carelessly. Deciphering his meaning had always been a bit of a chore. But these — these were painstakingly produced without a single blot or smear, and the characters were carefully formed.

Presently, Bingley stood to the side, watching Jane until, finally, she looked his way and smiled at him. Within moments, he was at her side and had taken her hand in his.

"They are happy," Elizabeth whispered as she leaned toward Darcy. "I am glad of it."

"As am I." Darcy took her hand and, placing it in the crook of his elbow, held it there as he led her past Lord Matlock, who was in what sounded to be a serious discussion with Mr. Amberly.

"You are leaving so soon?" asked Georgiana with a twinkle in her eye. "But what of your guests?" She crossed her arms and feigned a glare at her brother.

"You are capable of seeing to them," he answered.

She sighed and attempted to hide her smile. "At least, it is more entertaining than looking at carriages."

He chuckled and gave her forehead a kiss. Then, with a nod toward a certain gentleman and with a teasing smile of his own, he said, "Please inform Mr. Murrish that I would be pleased to meet with him whenever he comes to his senses, so long as that does not happen for at least a week's time."

Georgiana's cheeks grew rosy. "You find him acceptable?"

"I do."

Georgiana smiled and thanked him before moving toward the man whom Darcy had indicated.

"He is a fine man, and she seems quite fond of him," said Darcy with a last look at his sister before leaving the room with Elizabeth.

"She will be happy with him," agreed Elizabeth. Elizabeth knew that Darcy's sister was a good deal more than just fond of the gentleman. Georgiana had shared a great deal with Elizabeth about Mr. Murrish, including her fear that her brother might not approve of the match since, although Mr. Murrish's income was good, it was not grand. It was not a matter of fearing she would marry beneath her station. Standing in society had long ago become of little importance to her brother, but she knew he would fear she would not be content to live in a smaller home with less fine things.

"I believe she will be," he agreed as they climbed the stairs. Reaching the landing where the staircase turned to continue its climb to the family's rooms, he paused to give her a brief, soft kiss.

"Are you happy, Mrs. Darcy?" he asked as they continued up the few remaining stairs.

Elizabeth leaned into his arm and squeezed it tightly. "Ask me again," she said as both her feet reached the top of the stairs.

He smiled down at her. "Are you happy, Mrs. Darcy?"

She nodded. "However, it is such a small word that I am not convinced it can contain the depth of my joy."

He agreed and bent to kiss her lightly once again.

She smiled at him, and before he could straighten completely, she drew his face down to hers, so that she might kiss him as she had that night in the garden at the ball. It was a kiss which now, as it did then, caused desire to swirl and dance within her.

Wrapping his arms around her, Darcy pulled her close. Delight filled him. She was his, at last. "Elizabeth," he whispered as he pressed kisses along her neck. "My Elizabeth."

She sighed and held him tightly to her. "Your Mrs. Darcy," she whispered. She felt him smile against her neck at the comment as he continued his trail of kisses up her neck and along her jaw before claiming her lips once again.

A dish clattered to the floor somewhere below them, and breaking their kiss, he scooped her into his arms to carry her to their room. "My Mrs. Darcy," he said as he kissed her forehead. "Finally, my Mrs. Darcy."

Epilogue

Sparks leapt toward the chimney as the yule log hissed and popped. Elizabeth snuggled a bit more closely to her husband. Little Thomas Alexander Darcy's fist dropped from his mouth, and he whimpered softly as he rubbed his nose on his papa's shoulder before turning his face away and returning to peaceful sleeping. He had been born only six months ago. There would be no season for Elizabeth this year. She and Darcy would happily wile away their time in the country watching their precious son grow. Darcy could not be happier to be missing the season, and fortunately, Mr. Murrish had finally come to him and offered for Georgiana. They were happily married and expecting a child in the spring. Their residence, of course, was in London, but tonight and for the last fortnight and at least another one to follow, depending on the weather, they were ensconced along with a large gathering of family at Pemberley.

"I should say not," Colonel Fitzwilliam's voice boomed across the room. His lovely wife, Arabella, the sister of a Spanish colonel whom he had worked alongside as an aide de camp during the occupation, raised a delicate brow and spoke softly to him in her native tongue. He nodded to Darcy and smiled sheepishly at Elizabeth in apology. Then, he turned to the group gathered around him to continue his tale about some happening from his time in France.

He had arrived at Pemberley just last week. He had accompanied his commander back from the continent with the last of the troops at the end of November, and then, after a short time in London settling into his townhouse and making ready his office for the beginning of the parliamentary season, he had been given leave to travel.

"He has survived well," Darcy commented. It was not the first time he had said so since Richard's arrival.

"I am sure there are shadows," Elizabeth replied. "There always are."

Darcy clasped her hand in his. He knew she

was not only speaking of shadows formed by the atrocities of war but also of the shadows that hung about any individual after a trying experience — fears, guilt, regrets, or the dreaded expectation of the recurrence of some event.

"They can be vanquished," he whispered.

Her head rubbed against his shoulder as she nodded. "Most can, but I imagine there are particularly dark ones which cannot." She squeezed his hand. "I am glad that no such shadows have attached themselves to our family."

"As am I." He shifted slightly as his foot began to prickle from sitting in one position for so long. "I fear the shadow over Bingley may never rise."

Elizabeth smiled and lifted his hand to her lips. "You are a very good man, Mr. Darcy."

"Thank you," he turned his head to look down at her, "but I am not entirely certain as to the reason for my goodness."

"You care for him," she smiled up at Darcy and tilted her head toward where Bingley and Jane sat listening to Richard's tale. "A lesser man would not."

"You give me too much credit, my dear."

She chuckled. "I do no such thing, sir. I have

watched you not only forgive the one who so grievously wronged you, but you have also taken care to ensure he knows that he is forgiven. No mention of his wrong doings has crossed your lips in his presence," she lifted a brow, "even when he has been particularly trying about something." She sighed. "I do not know how Jane tolerates his stubbornness at times."

At that, Darcy chuckled, and Thomas once again whimpered and turned his head, apparently unhappy with the rumbling of the laugh. "I imagine she learned patience from you," he lowered his voice and a particularly attractive, if somewhat impish, smile played at his mouth, "as well as your other sisters and mother."

Elizabeth attempted to scowl but could not. He was correct. Jane was the only one who ever responded with patience to any of her sisters or her mother. Nearly all of those trying Bennet women were in attendance at Pemberley. Elizabeth sighed contentedly.

Mrs. Bennet was currently in the nursery reading stories to Jane's children. Nothing, not even the colonel's tales of far of places, would dissuade her from what she saw as her responsibilities as a grandmother.

Mary had not journeyed to Derbyshire. Her husband's business could not be shut up, and she would not leave him to manage alone, especially not at Christmas.

Lydia had attempted to be included in the group, but no invitation had been extended. A parcel of presents and a bit of money had, however, found their way to the Wickhams in Newcastle. Jane had heard of the package being assembled and had made certain a warm pair of woolen socks for each of Lydia's two daughters, as well as a new cap for Lydia, were included.

Kitty was in attendance, but she was not especially merry, for she had left behind her beau, who, just prior to her leaving, had made an offer for her hand and was accepted. She was finding the separation to be a trial, but an unlikely source — Bingley — had often come to her aid in diverting her with a game or some small bit of amusement. And so, she was tolerating her sojourn in Derbyshire with a greater sense of equanimity that Elizabeth had foreseen.

Darcy shifted beside her again. "We should see

Thomas to his bed," he suggested. "I do believe Uncle Amberly is about to snore."

The gentleman's head was bowed, and his eye closed.

"You know he is waiting to see the child to his bed and kiss his head."

It had become a tradition of sorts during the Amberly's short stay at Pemberley. Each night, as Thomas was carried to his bed, Gareth Amberly would follow behind and, after Darcy and Elizabeth had said their good nights, he would whisper a poem to the boy, kiss his head, and place a coin in a jar to pay the maker of dreams for pleasant ones.

Maria Amberly would shake her head and smile as she watched. They had had no children on which to dote, save Jack when he came to them. And so, they doted on Thomas as grandparents would, and neither Darcy nor Elizabeth discouraged it. For without Uncle Amberly's interference, the wiggly, often demanding child, who was sleeping on Darcy's shoulder, would not have come to be.

"We should" Elizabeth stood and offered her hand to help Darcy rise from the couch. "We will return," she assured Lady Matlock, who had turned to look in their direction. The comment was greeted with a tentative smile and a small nod.

Lady Matlock had yet to be completely won over in her opinion of Elizabeth, but she kept her peace and refrained from any disparagement and slowly seemed to be coming around to the position that her husband had already adopted that Elizabeth was quite acceptable and decidedly charming.

After seeing their son to bed, Darcy drew Elizabeth down the hall and to the window in their room to look out at the clear star-filled sky. He wrapped her in his arms, pulling her against his chest and kissing the top of her head. "It is peaceful," he murmured.

Elizabeth sighed and relaxed against him. "Will you be wishing on a Christmas star, Mr. Darcy?"

"I might." He kissed the top of her head again. "But it will not be for me."

She turned to look at him. "It will not? Then, for whom shall it be?"

He brushed a piece of hair from her face. "Thomas, perhaps."

She smiled at him. "And for what will you wish?"

"That he shall one day be as happy as I am at this very moment with a house filled with family who are safe and well and a wife whom I adore." He kissed her softly. "And you Mrs. Darcy, for what would you wish?"

She pursed her lips and furrowed her brow. "I would wish happiness for our children, but it seems you have already done so if you but change the wording to include more than just Thomas."

Darcy chuckled. "Very well, I shall include all of our children in my wish."

"Then, I have nothing left for which to wish, for the desire of my heart, whom I once thought was lost, now holds me in his arms and speaks of our children." She smiled as Darcy cupped her face in his hands and kissed her.

He kissed her while down the hall, past the nursery, Uncle Amberly climbed into his bed where he could snore in peace, and Aunt Amberly prepared to endure it.

He kissed her while beneath them, in a crowded sitting room, as Richard began another tale of far away places, Jane slipped her hand into Bingley's and smiled, not as she always did, but just for him.

Though Elizabeth reminded him of their guests, Darcy continued to kiss her, even as Lady Matlock glanced at the clock before frowning at the door to the sitting room, and Lord Matlock patted her hand and gave her a wink.

"I said we would return," Elizabeth attempted a second weak protest as Darcy's mouth left her lips, turning their attention to her neck just below her ear.

"Mmm hmm," he murmured, "we will."

And they did, but not until they had made certain that, next Christmas, there would be more than just Thomas for whom to wish.

Acknowledgements

There are many who have had a part in the creation of this story. Some have read and commented on it. Some have proofread for grammatical errors and plot holes. Others have not even read the story (and a few, I know, will never read it), but their encouragement and belief in my ability, as well as their patience when I became cranky or when supper was late or the groceries ran low, was invaluable.

And so, I would like to say *thank you* to Zoe, Rose, Betty, Kristine, Ben, and Kyle, as well as the lovely readers at darcyandlizzy.com. Because of some of you, this story is better. It now has an epilogue and a prologue and fewer grammatical errors. Because of all of you, I feel blessed through your help, support, and understanding.

I have not listed my dear husband in the above group because, to me, he deserves his own special thank you, for without his somewhat pushy insistence that I start sharing my writing, none of my writing goals and dreams would have been met.

Choices Series

HER FATHER'S CHOICE

Book 1 in the Choices Series
Sometimes a father knows what is best for his child. At least Mr. Bennet trusts he does. Seeing the potential of a good match for his beloved Lizzy but knowing her ability to hold a grudge, he puts a plan into action that forces a marriage between Darcy and Elizabeth.

NO OTHER CHOICE

Book 2 in the Choices Series
Mary Bennet has never been the center of attention and rarely the object of any man's affections, but that is about to change. Shortly after Darcy and Elizabeth's wedding, Mary travels to London to prepare for the season, a season she is

determined to finish with either a husband or a glorious tale to tell, even if it means learning to tolerate Lord Rycroft.

HIS INCONVENIENT CHOICE

Book 3 in the Choices Series
Colonel Fitzwilliam has always known his father would try to force him into a marriage of convenience, but after Kitty Bennet captures his heart as she shivered in the cold on the streets of Meryton, he realizes his only chance at happiness lies in making an inconvenient choice. However, it is a choice that will not go unchallenged, and as family secrets are revealed, it is a choice that, in creating happiness for the colonel, could destroy his family.

HER HEART'S CHOICE

Book 4 in the Choices Series
To Anne, it had seemed simple enough. Place an advertisement in the paper, interview the gentlemen who responded, and select the best husband. But nothing is as easy as it seems. Indeed,

many things are quite the opposite of how they appear. How is a lady to find a safe and secure marriage when her ideals are turned on their head — especially when her heart yearns for a man who is wholly unsuitable?

Other Books by Leenie Brown

OXFORD COTTAGE

Elizabeth Bennet expects to complete the challenge her father has set before her at Oxford Cottage. What she does not expect is to meet a handsome stranger and fall in love, nor does she expect to find herself in a situation where she will have to keep both herself and her young companion safe.

FOR PEACE OF MIND

After refusing Mr. Collins' offer of marriage, Elizabeth Bennet is sent to stay with her aunt and uncle in London. While there, she finds both love and opposition. Can she keep both her love and her peace of mind?

LISTEN TO YOUR HEART

When Anne de Bourgh finds some hidden papers, her view of the future changes in light of her father's wishes.

Her declaration to follow her heart and choose her own future causes discord and forces secrets to be revealed. Sometimes the path to happily ever after can be strewn with danger and intrigue.

THROUGH EVERY STORM

Wickham is a changed man, but his wife has yet to leave some of her childish ways behind. Can a former wastrel redeem both himself and his wife?

TEATIME TALES

A collection of six short and sweet Jane Austen-inspired stories intended to be a light pick-me-up.

AND THEN LOVE

A Pride and Prejudice Prequel
and
A Willow Hall Romance
Events from the past combined with threats in
the present threaten to tear Lucy and Philip apart
unless Darcy can help his friends save their blos-
soming love and rid Lucy of her uncle once and
for all.

About the Author

Leenie Brown has always been a girl with an active imagination, which, while growing up, was a both an asset, providing many hours of fun as she played out stories, and a liability, when her older sister and aunt would tell her frightening tales. At one time, they had her convinced Dracula lived in the trunk at the end of the bed she slept in when visiting her grandparents!

Although it has been years since she cowered in her bed in her grandparents' basement, she still has an imagination which occasionally runs away with her, and she feeds it now as she did then — by reading!

Her heroes, when growing up, were authors, and the worlds they painted with words were (and still are) her favourite playgrounds! She was that child, under the covers with the flashlight, reading until the wee hours of the morning...and pretending not to be tired the next day so her mother wouldn't find out.

In addition to feeding her imagination, she also exercises it — by writing. While writing has been an activity she has dabbled in over the years, it blossomed into a full-fledged obsession when she stumbled upon the world of Jane Austen Fan Fiction. Leenie had first fallen in love with Jane Austen's work in her early teens when she was captivated by the tale of a girl, who like her, was the second born of five daughters. Now, as an adult, she spends much time in the regency world, playing with the characters from her favourite Jane Austen novels and a few that are of her own creation.

When she is not traipsing down a trail in an attempt to keep up with her imagination, Leenie resides in the beautiful province of Nova Scotia with her two sons and her very own Mr. Brown (a wonderful mix of all the best of Darcy, Bingley and Edmund with a healthy dose of the teasing Mr. Tilney and just a dash of the scolding Mr. Knightley).

Connect with Leenie Brown

E-mail:

LeenieBrownAuthor@gmail.com

Twitter:

@LeenieBAuthor

Facebook:

www.facebook.com/LeenieBrownAuthor

Blog:

leeniebrown.com

Subscribe to Leenie's Mailing List:

Book News from Leenie Brown

(http://eepurl.com/bSieI1)

Join Leenie on Austen Authors:

austenauthors.net

60140623R00078

Made in the USA
Lexington, KY
28 January 2017